DRAC'S IN LOVE!

Adapted by Cala Spinner
Illustrated by Adam Devaney

Ready-to-Read

Simon Spotlight
New York   London   Toronto   Sydney   New Delhi

SIMON SPOTLIGHT
An imprint of Simon & Schuster Children's Publishing Division
1230 Avenue of the Americas, New York, New York 10020
This Simon Spotlight edition June 2018
TM & © 2018 Sony Pictures Animation Inc. All Rights Reserved.
All rights reserved, including the right of reproduction in whole or in part in any form.
SIMON SPOTLIGHT, READY-TO-READ, and colophon are registered trademarks of Simon & Schuster, Inc.
For information about special discounts for bulk purchases, please contact Simon & Schuster Special Sales
at 1-866-506-1949 or business@simonandschuster.com.
Manufactured in the United States of America 0418 LAK
10 9 8 7 6 5 4 3 2 1
ISBN 978-1-5344-1835-6 (hc)
ISBN 978-1-5344-1834-9 (pbk)
ISBN 978-1-5344-1836-3 (eBook)

Have you heard of a Zing?
A Zing is an important thing.
It happens when you
meet your soul mate.
Drac felt a Zing when he met
his wife, Martha.

Martha and Drac were very happy.
They had a daughter named Mavis.
But then Martha died.
Drac was determined to be
the best dad ever.
He loved taking care of Mavis.

More than one hundred years passed.
Mavis grew up.
She Zinged with a human named
Johnny. They married
and had a son, Dennis.
Drac adored his grandson!

Drac's friends wanted him
to meet someone new to love.
Drac disagreed.
His life was full.

He had his family
and the hotel.
What else did he need?

But soon Drac began to think it might be nice to meet some new monsters.

Mavis had a surprise for the family.
Even though they all worked at
the hotel, they never got to
spend time together having fun.
So she booked a vacation
for all of them.
A monster cruise!

When Drac explored the boat,
he saw stairs, ocean views,
and monsters playing games.
It was beautiful.
He was happy to be here
with his family.

Then Drac saw a woman.
It was the ship's captain.
Their eyes met.
Much to Drac's surprise,
he Zinged!

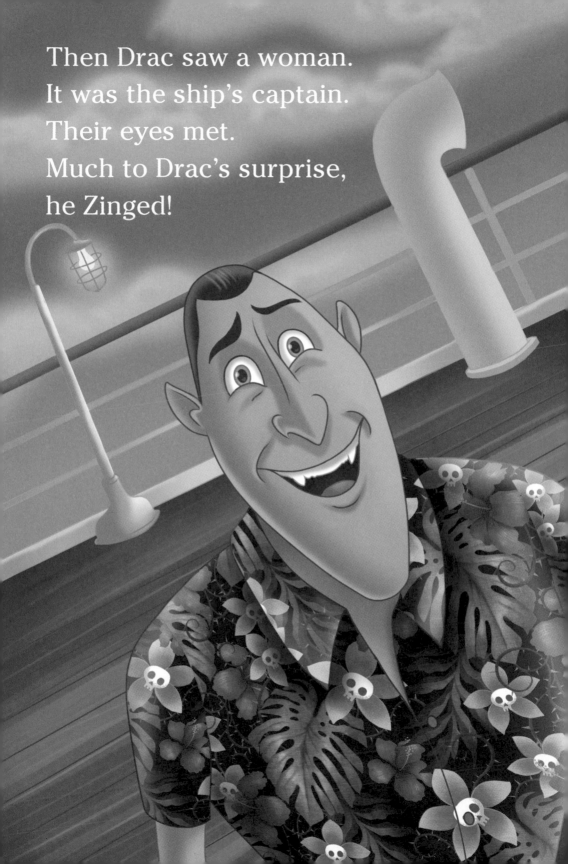

Drac was shocked.
He was in love!
The woman's name
was Ericka.
She was a human.

Mavis didn't trust Ericka. Something about her seemed strange.

Ericka was a monster hunter.
Her great-grandfather was
Abraham Van Helsing, the most
famous monster hunter of all time.
Drac was in love, but Ericka
wanted to kill Drac!

One night Ericka tried to kill
Drac by feeding him garlic.
But garlic doesn't kill vampires,
it makes them gassy!
Drac let out a big TOOT!

Drac was embarrassed.
He apologized to Ericka.
He told her that he hadn't been
on a date in a long time.
He didn't know what to do.

Ericka was surprised.
She didn't realize how much
monsters care for their families.
They had a lot in common!
She started to see Drac in a
different light.

Then Drac saved Ericka's life.
She was secretly trying to steal
a magical device that would destroy all
monsters, but she almost got
hurt instead.

Drac wanted his daughter to know
how he felt.
He told Mavis how he Zinged
when he saw Ericka.

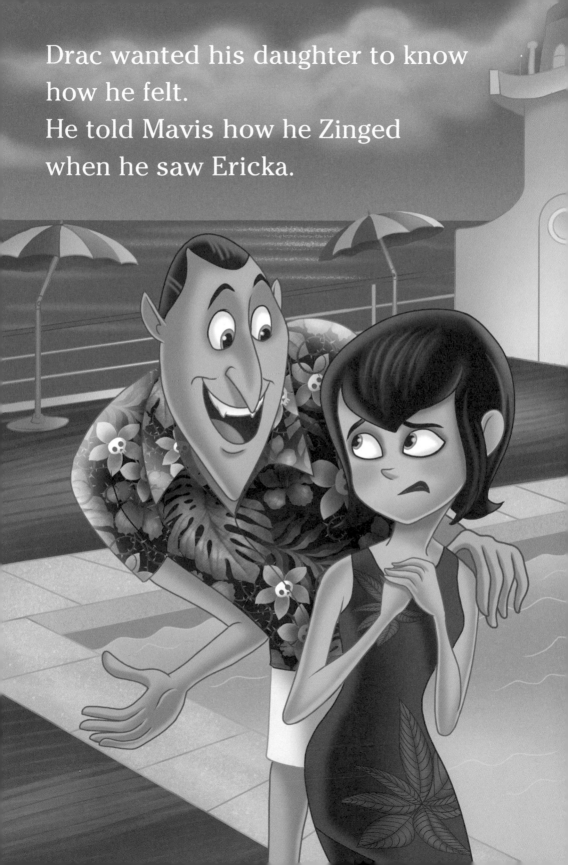

Mavis was shocked.
She had no idea her father
was looking for love.

Johnny told Mavis that she
had to let her dad be happy.
Mavis finally understood.
After all, you can't deny a Zing.

Mavis told Drac to find Ericka.
He needed to say that he loved her.
He hoped that she'd be able to love
him too.

Drac found Ericka in a DJ booth.
She was with someone.
It was her great-grandfather,
Abraham Van Helsing!

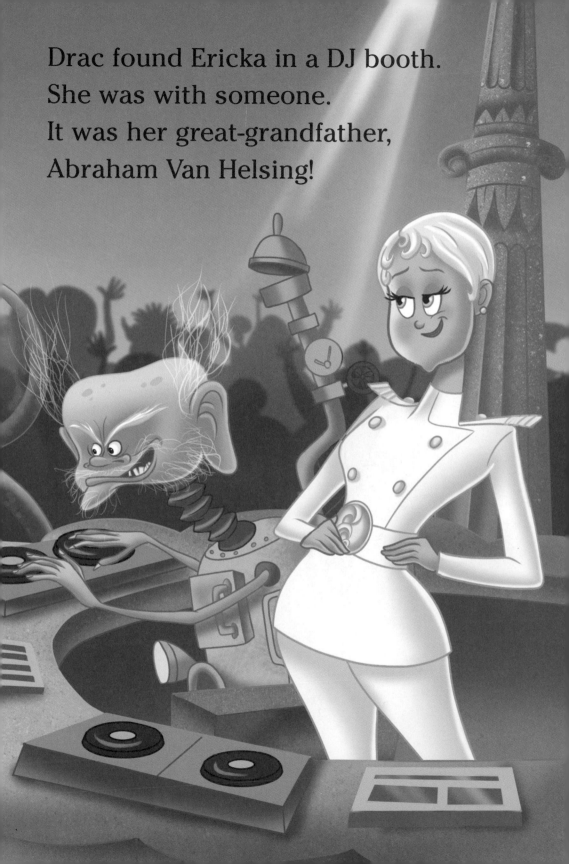

Before Drac knew it,
Van Helsing started his plan.
He activated the device that would
destroy all the monsters.

A sea monster appeared,
and it grabbed Mavis and Drac!

It seemed like the monsters
were done for.

But then Ericka jumped in!
This time, it was *Ericka*
who saved *Drac*!

"You're wrong about monsters,"
Ericka told her great-grandfather.
"Monsters love, just like we do."

Then Ericka said something amazing.
When she first saw Drac,
she had Zinged too!

The monsters defeated Van Helsing's
plan, but Drac made sure
that Van Helsing was safe.
You see, not too long ago,
Drac was scared of humans.
He saw that Van Helsing was
just scared of monsters.

Drac realized the more he
learned about Van Helsing, the
more they were the same.
Ericka was happy.
She looked at
Drac and they
Zinged again!

A Zing is a special feeling.
It can happen more than once.
If you are lucky, someday
you will Zing just like
Mavis and Johnny
or Ericka and Drac!